# Brother Wolf of Gubbio

A
LEGEND
OF
SAINT FRANCIS

WRITTEN
AND ILLUSTRATED BY
Colony Elliott Santangelo

 Handprint Books

Text and illustrations copyright © 2000 by Colony Elliott Santangelo

All rights reserved

Published by Handprint Books, Inc.

413 Sixth Avenue

Brooklyn,

New York 11215

www.handprintbooks.com

Library of Congress Cataloging-in-Publication Data

Santangelo, Colony Elliott.

Brother Wolf of Gubbio: a legend of Saint Francis / written and illustrated by Colony
Elliott Santangelo.--1st ed.

p.cm.

Summary: An old and hungry wolf terrorizes the townspeople of Gubbio until Saint
Francis shows the villagers how to live peacefully with the wolf.

ISBN: 1-929766-07-6

[1. Wolves--fiction. 2. Francis, of Assisi, Saint, 1182-1226--Fiction.] I. Title

PZ7.S238115 Br 2000

[Fic]--dc21                                                                                  00-037011

Printed and bound in China

The text of this book has been set in 16pt ITC Kallos Medium. The display has been set in Goudy Text Lombardic.

The illustrations were prepared using inks and colored pencils on bass wood panels.

Book design by Martha Rago

ISBN: 1-929766-07-6

First Edition

10 9 8 7 6 5 4 3 2 1

To my two most enduring supporters:

My daughter Bronwen,
who inspired me
to begin all those years ago,
and my husband Robert,
who has made it possible
to continue all these years now.

And in memory of my stepson, Rocco,
who was the real artist in the family.

# The town of Gubbio

is built along the side of Monte Ingino
in the Umbrian region of Italy. Overlooking the buildings,
near the top of the mountain, is the church of Saint Ubaldo,
the patron saint of the town.  But once upon a time
another saint came to Gubbio.

And so did a wolf.

**O**nce, a very long time ago, a pack of wolves searched for a place that would provide shelter and good hunting. The wolves journeyed until they came to Gubbio, a small town built on a mountainside. There was a smell of forest and fur that came from the other side of the mountain. So they followed the green, furry smell to their new forest home.

But not all the wolves went over the mountain that night. One wolf crawled off the path. Once he had been the leader of the pack. Now he was old and tired, and a new, young leader had taken his place.

The wolf put his head down and closed his eyes.

The next morning a shepherd herded his sheep to pasture. The wolf was awakened by the rumbling of his empty belly. He saw a lamb and trembled with hunger. Here was a meal right in front of him!

So, summoning the last of his strength, the wolf leaped up, pounced on the lamb, and ate it.

That evening the shepherd went searching for his lost lamb. He soon found the remains of the wolf's meal. The shepherd studied the pawprints, then looked up in wonder and fear. Wolves? On the mountain?

Over the next few weeks another lamb disappeared.
Then three chickens.
Then a goat.

The shepherd told the baker about the prints he had seen. The baker told the butcher, and before long each man in town boasted loudly that *he* would climb the mountain and hunt down the wolves!
But no one did.

Market day came, and the piazza was filled with people. The lonely wolf, hearing the excitement, was curious, so he followed the mountain path to town.

The wolf crawled from house to house until he was right behind the butcher's stall. The smell of meat was so delicious that he forgot to be careful.

A little girl saw him first. She gasped. Her mother and father looked up. The baker and the butcher and the shepherd all turned around.

"Wolves!" the shepherd cried.

Now everyone saw him.

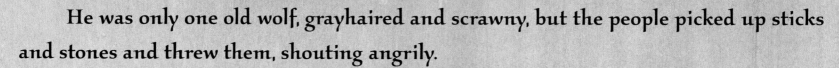

He was only one old wolf, grayhaired and scrawny, but the people picked up sticks and stones and threw them, shouting angrily.

The wolf roared in pain, and the people shouted even louder. Then they ran into their homes, and the wolf ran out of Gubbio.

From that day the war between the wolf and the people of Gubbio grew worse. The wolf snatched another lamb, and the shepherd was afraid to take his sheep to pasture anymore. So the wolf came into town again, looking for chickens to keep his belly full.

Soon the townspeople were too fearful to leave their homes.

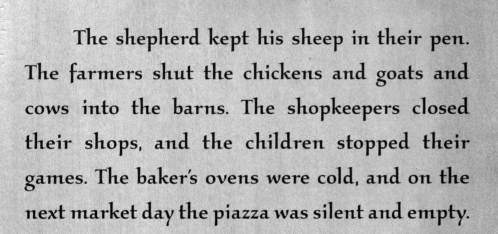

The shepherd kept his sheep in their pen. The farmers shut the chickens and goats and cows into the barns. The shopkeepers closed their shops, and the children stopped their games. The baker's ovens were cold, and on the next market day the piazza was silent and empty.

Finally the baker grew tired of being afraid. He wanted to walk in the streets and see his friends. He wanted to fire his ovens and bake bread! "There is only one man who can help us," he said to himself, "and I am going to bring him here."

And so the baker crept out and ran through the town until he reached the road that led out of Gubbio.

Down that road
was the town of Assisi. For days
now the people of Assisi had talked about
the fearsome monster that terrorized their
neighbors in Gubbio. One man, however,
said nothing but listened to all that was said.
This man was Francis, and everyone who
knew him called him a holy man. Long ago
Francis had given away his riches and chosen
to spend his life celebrating the beauty of the
world and the brotherhood of all living
things. He was gentle and loving with the
sick and the poor, and he shared what little he
had with anyone who was in need, even birds
and forest animals. Francis was a man so full
of joy that many who saw him longed to be
near him and follow his example.

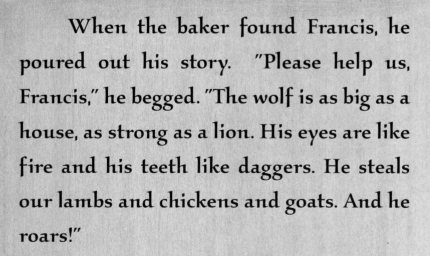

When the baker found Francis, he poured out his story. "Please help us, Francis," he begged. "The wolf is as big as a house, as strong as a lion. His eyes are like fire and his teeth like daggers. He steals our lambs and chickens and goats. And he roars!"

Francis said, "Of course he roars. He is a wolf, and you threw stones at him. Yes, I will come with you."

So Francis and the baker returned to Gubbio. Patiently Francis listened to the people. Then he said, "My brothers and sisters, when Brother Wolf is hungry, he must eat, just like you. But a wolf hunts whatever he can, even lambs and chickens and goats. He is only doing what wolves do. Now I must find the wolf."

The people beseeched Francis not to go. "Even you, good brother, will not tame this monster. He is sure to eat you!" they said.

But Francis shook his head, smiling, and walked out of Gubbio until he reached the wolf's lair.

"Brother Wolf," he called gently, "come out and greet me. I have no sticks and stones to throw. I do not shout. I stand on the same ground as you, and the sun that warms me has light enough for us both."

The wolf had never heard a voice like this, one so soft and tender that it stirred something hidden and almost forgotten deep within him. This voice sounded like one of his own, like family. Slowly, he crawled out of his lair.

"Well, you are no fearsome monster, are you?" said Francis. "You have only hunted so you could eat, as wolves do. But Brother Wolf, you have also frightened people and hunted the animals upon which they depend. Listen now. If the people of Gubbio promise to feed and care for you all the rest of your days, will you promise never to harm another living creature? Will you live peacefully under the same sun and moon and stars with all your brothers and sisters?"

rancis raised his arms, and the wolf felt a great joy fill him until there was no room left for hunger or fear.

Then Francis said, "Brother Wolf, here is my hand. Show me your pledge of good faith to live in harmony with the people of Gubbio from now on."

And the wolf did as Francis bid him.

When Francis and the wolf returned to Gubbio, the wolf once again pledged his good faith. The people exclaimed in wonder, saying that Francis had brought them a miracle.

"Not I," said Francis. "The miracle is what makes the wolf your brother."

The townspeople promised to do as Francis asked. The baker was the first to approach the wolf.

"You come with me, brother," he whispered. "I will bake a nice, big, buttery loaf of bread just for you."

And that is the story of how the wolf of Gubbio became Brother Wolf of Gubbio. For two years the wolf lived as a member of every family in town. His belly was never empty, and his fur grew rich and glossy as the children took turns brushing him. He joined in their games and guarded all the people in their daily comings and goings.

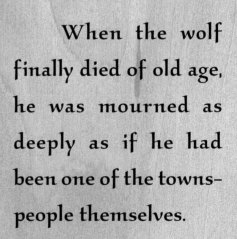

When the wolf finally died of old age, he was mourned as deeply as if he had been one of the towns-people themselves.

Which, if you asked the people of Gubbio, he had indeed become.